For my niece, Alex, who helped me to realize that this was possible and to everyone who ever believed in me. Thank you and enjoy...

-MMD

"The storm is approaching us faster than we think. Hurricane Jude will be here before we know it. Please make sure you are taking the proper precautions." The TV weather lady sounded worried. "Please do not take this storm lightly. It's going to be one of the biggest we've experienced yet." I lay curled up safely at the foot of Shelby's bed.

"It's going to be okay, Sandy," Shelby said to me. My nerves were setting in and I was starting to shake. Shelby calmed me down, though. She always does. I knew she'd look after me. She gave me a gentle pat on the head and a tight, comforting hug. Ugh, I love her hugs.

Shelby is my best friend and my number one priority. She is ten years old and suffers from a disease called epilepsy. Epilepsy causes Shelby to have frequent seizures. When Shelby has a seizure, she falls unconscious and starts shaking uncontrollably. Seizures are very scary. Luckily, I've been trained to assist her during and after her seizures. I know when she's about to have one and I get her mom to give her the medication that helps with them. I'm proud of how well I look after Shelby when she needs me. She deserves it! She's basically the most awesome person ever.

Shelby and I live together in a beautiful home in the Southernmost part of Florida, along with Shelby's mom, Kelly and her four-year-old brother, Luke. Shelby's dad left the family when Luke was only a couple of months old, so Shelby's mom has raised both of her kids on her own. Luke doesn't like me all that much, probably because I spend most of my time with Shelby.

Shelby and I do everything together. I have to be by her side in case she has a seizure. Going to school is by far my favorite thing to do. Watching her with all her friends is amazing and recess and lunch are to die for. All of the teachers at school know me by name and sometimes give me treats which is a definite plus! When the weather is nice, Shelby and I walk to the school together because it's only a couple blocks away from our house. We haven't been able to walk lately, though. We've been drenched with bucketloads of rain over the past few days because of the nearing storm.

I've been hearing more and more talk about this hurricane and it's really starting to freak me out. I've heard about hurricanes before, but never experienced one. This week at school, we learned a lot about them. They bring high winds and heavy rain. They can even destroy houses, bring down trees, and cause flash flooding. We read stories about past hurricanes and all of the people who lost their houses. I was sad and afraid that Hurricane Jude would cause damage to our house.

At least Kelly was preparing us for the absolute worst. As soon as she heard that there was the slightest possibility of a hurricane, she started packing bags full of clothes and food for Shelby and Luke. She made all of the necessary phone calls and spoke with all of our neighbors, including the Johnson's next door. She had a plan. When the hurricane hit our area, we were going to climb into the Johnsons' boat and float safely to a nearby shelter where we could stay until the storm was over.

I went over the plan in my head as the winds picked up and before I knew it, I was whimpering in fear. Shelby was already fast asleep. She looked peaceful, her arms curled around Candy, her pink and white teddy bear. I crawled up to the head of Shelby's bed, wanting to be close to her. I rested my head on her pillow as I listened to the rain violently pelting our roof. I just wanted the storm to end. I wanted sunny days and warm walks to school again.

I must have fallen asleep because the next thing I knew, Shelby was screaming my name and shaking me, "Sandy! Please wake up! We have to go."

I opened my eyes and found Shelby standing in front of me

with her bag in her hand and her yellow raincoat on. This was it. The storm was hitting. I leapt from the bed and into her arms, shaking like a leaf. The wind whirled, thunder crashed, and lots of water flooded into our house. I didn't know what to do, but I tried to be strong for Shelby. Kelly led the way, car-rying Luke in one arm and the bags she'd packed in the other. Shelby followed closely behind and carried me with her. The water was rising.

"Mommy, I'm scared," I heard Luke say as we tried to get into the Johnsons' boat.
"It's going to be okay," Kelly replied gently. She loaded him into the boat and zipped his blue life jacket tightly.
Shelby put me down in the boat. I shivered. My paws and legs were soaked.
"Sorry for getting you wet, Sandy," Shelby said. I lay down by her feet. I didn't care about my wet paws, I was just glad that we were all together and safe.

We were all scared, bunched up together and bobbing along in the boat. Then, the sky gave a loud crash as thunder rolled overhead. A huge wave hit our boat. BOOM! CRASH! The boat rocked violently.

Luke was at the edge of the boat. The giant wave took him by surprise. He toppled out and very quickly began to be carried away by the rushing water that was underneath us.
"No!" Shelby screamed. Kelly rushed to the edge of the boat,

trying to reach Luke and pull him back to safety. I jumped up from my spot at Shelby's feet and looked over the edge of the boat. Luke was trying his hardest to swim. His life jacket could barely keep him afloat. I knew what I had to do.

SPLASH! Into the freezing cold water I went, and then under the water, trying to work out which way was up so that I could breathe again. Luke struggled against the waves. I swam like I didn't know I could and, finally, I reached him. Grabbing Luke by his life jacket, I pulled and tugged him back towards the boat, trying my best to keep his head above water. We went under a couple of times and at one point I didn't think we were going to be coming back up. The water was so cold that, when we finally reached the safety of the boat, my paws had gone all blue and tingly. Kelly and Shelby grabbed Luke from me when we were close enough, lifting him safely back into the boat a draping towel around his shaking shoulders. He was screaming and crying. Noticing that I was still in the water, Mrs. Johnson raced to Luke's aid and Kelly leaned over the edge of the boat to grab my paw. I tried to climb up, but it was too slippery. Thunder clapped again. Another wave crashed into me. Kelly lost her grip on my paw and I sunk down into the water.

I gasped for air, trying my hardest not to let the water keep me down. The boat bobbed up and down and began to drift away "Sandy!" Shelby cried.

I started to float down the river. I tried so hard to swim back toward the boat to get back to Shelby, but the water was rushing faster than I could paddle. Waves crashed over my head and the boat grew smaller and smaller. I was stranded. The wind too strong, forcing me back underwater each time I managed to right myself. I sunk once more and when I came up, the boat disappeared into the distance. I started to cry.

Out of the corner of my eye, I saw something floating close to me. I went towards it. It was only a milk crate, but it would have to do. I climbed in and started floating down the river sad and alone.

Chapter 2

After being dragged down the river for what felt like hours, my crate got caught on a broken tree limb. Soaking wet I managed to crawl up onto somewhat dry land. The sun set, and the sky was pitch black. I trudged towards a dark alley filled with trash cans. Knocking one over, I laid down in a smelly pile of junk.

Hoping that my family were safe, I closed my eyes and slowly drifted into a restless sleep.

In my dreams, the hurricane never struck. Shelby was still by my side, laughing and smiling as we played in the yard. Kelly brought out some icecream for her and, like always, Shelby let me have a lick. Luke was playing in his sandbox and Shelby was throwing the ball for me. Everything was peaceful and right.

CRASH! I jolted awake. My eyes opened wide.

What was that? Trying my hardest to be brave, I slowly peeked my head out of the trash can and, to my surprise, found that I was not alone. Grubby-handed and naughty, a filthy raccoon rummaged through the garbage can he just knocked over. I came out of my can with a large piece of bright pink bubble gum stuck in my fur. Ick! He shot me a disgusted look. "Hello," I said, trying to be friendly. He ignored me and contin-ued to dig through the trash. I chuckled nervously. "It's a nice day out today, considering that storm last night." The raccoon still didn't answer. Carefully, I walked closer towards him. He glared at me again and finally broke his silence. "What on earth are you doing in MY trash?" "What?" I asked. "You heard me. This is MY trash!" The raccoon's voice got louder and louder. "I'm sorry, I had nowhere else to go," I told him. "Why not?" He demanded, and without waiting for an answer, he said, "For the last time, this is my territory. You need to hop off, seriously, lady." "You don't have to be so mean," I bristled. "I said I was sorry." "Look, lady, I just want to eat in peace so keep it moving." "Okay, okay." I said. "I was just leaving. I'm sorry again." "Why are you even here?" The raccoon asked, munching on a half-eaten piece of moldy cheese. Putting my disgust aside, I started to explain my situation. "The hurricane last night flooded my house and after being pushed around in an awful flood, this is where I washed up. Look, it's been a long night. I'm sorry, I didn't mean to be in your trash. I just needed a dry place to sleep."

"Huh, I see," said the raccoon. "I understand. I'm sorry for being rude to you. I was just hangry. I'm Ricky. Ricky the raccoon, at your service," he extended his paw as for me to shake it, I shook it gladly.

"Nice to meet you, Ricky. I'm Sandy. I'm a service dog for a girl named Shelby," I told him proudly. "Do you think you can help me get back to my family? I really miss Shelby and I need to be with her in case she has an episode." "An episode?" Ricky asked.

"Yes. Shelby has epilepsy. She has seizures at least a couple of times a week and I'm afraid that if I'm not there she might not be okay. Can you please help me get back to my family? I didn't sleep very well last night in that trash can without Shelby. Plus, I'm starving."

"I'd offer you my cheese, but I'm almost finished, and I don't share well with others," said Ricky.

"That's okay! Thanks for the offer, but I want to go home and eat there. Will you help me?" I pleaded.

"I'm sorry Sandy, I don't really know my way around Florida, I only moved here about a month ago," Ricky replied. Then he noticed the tears brimming in my eyes. "I might know someone who can help you find your way! His name is Max. He's an old friend of mine from back home and he's the reason I moved down here. He knows these streets like the back of his paw." "I'd love to meet him," I said eagerly. "Follow me," Ricky swallowed his last bite of cheese before setting off at a run.

Chapter 3

"Here we are," Ricky presented the worn-down backyard proudly, as if it was an amazing new amusement park. He seemed so genuine.

"Where exactly are we?" I asked. The backyard was fenced in and empty except for a small, crumbly house that looked like it hadn't been lived in for a long time. There was an in-ground swimming pool filled with muddy water and brown leaves and a chipped brown fence with broken boards and holes big enough to crawl through. I shook my head in disbelief and looked at Ricky who just shrugged. That's when Max appeared.

Covered in mud and carrying a steak bone that he must have rescued from the trash, Max was a grey scruffy-looking mutt with a whole lot of attitude. When he saw Ricky and I, he spun on his heel and started back towards the fence. "Where're ya going, Maxy?" Ricky called.

"I told you to never call me that," Max snarled. "What do you want?"

"Ooh, my man. Can't believe you went to T-Bones without me…again," Ricky pointed at the steak bone hanging out of Max's mouth.

"You weren't around, that's not my problem," he laughed. Max was definitely a few years older than me. His fur was matted, and he looked like he hadn't had a bath in months. He did have a ripped collar and name tag on, but there was no phone number or address. Poor thing. He looked like he could really use some love. "Who's your friend?" He spat, glaring at me.

"This is Sandy. Sandy the service dog," Ricky told him. I straightened my collar and tried to hide the pink gum in my fur.

"Oh, a service dog huh? I see. What's she doing with you?" Ricky shrugged so I stepped forward.

"I got separated from my family in the storm. I just want to go back home. Could you help me? Ricky said you know Florida well. I don't know where I am, I hate being outside longer than I have to be and I just want a nice, warm bath,"

"You're a service dog, aren't you?" Max growled. "You should know your way home, that's your job. You don't need me, figure it out for yourself."

"Max, can you at least try to be nice to Sandy? I like her," said Ricky. Max rolled his eyes.

"Thank you," I told Ricky, "and you," I looked at Max, "where do you get off with that attitude? I'm just trying to be nice. Please, I'm asking for your help."

"I know your type and you don't need my help," he said. I started to get angry.

"Excuse me? You have no right to..." I trailed off. I didn't wan to get on Max's bad side. What if he could still help me get back to Shelby?

"Go ahead and finish that thought. I'm interested in what you were going to say." He smirked. "No, I'm good, thanks."

"Come on. Rip into me. I'm waiting. You think you're so tough, but you're not. Girls aren't tough."

He stared at me with his big eyes and I found myself feeling sorry for him. I wondered how long he'd been on the streets with no family. Just a day in, I'm already losing my mind. I don't think I could do it forever.

"Don't pity me," Max broke the silence.

Woah. How did he know what I was thinking?

"Uh... I ... um," I stuttered.

"It's fine. I get it," he said.

"So, guys," Ricky clapped his hands together. "How about that weather? Pretty decent compared to last night's storm."

Max and I laughed and then Max seemed to decide something.

"Come on, let's get going," He led the way to the fence and climbed through the hole, Ricky at his heels. "What are you waiting for?"

At the other side of the fence was a big muddy puddle. This was no good. I already reeked.

"Is there another way around?" I asked quietly.

"What? Is the service princess afraid of a little mud?" Max laughed.

"No," I said defensively.

"Prove it." Mustering all my courage, I jumped through the hole like a champ and landed in the mud. No guy was going to tell me that I wasn't tough! Max was surprised I did it and he gently smiled.

"What city do you live in?" Max asked. "Homestead," I replied. "Where are we right now?" "We're up in Delray Beach. Not too far, but we better start walking sooner rather than later."

Like the three musketeers, we headed out as a team. Even though we'd only just met, I already felt connected to Max and Ricky. We walked for what felt like hours, playing games and heard thousands of Ricky's cheesy jokes. Listening to Ricky's loud and tuneless version of Taylor Swift's "We Are Never Getting Back Together" and feeling like we passed the same trees a hundred times, I saw something out of the cor-ner of my eye. There was a black and white cat digging a hole on the other side of the street.

"Look, a cat," I said as I started to walk towards it. "Maybe she can help us, too. I feel like we've been walking around in circles for hours. Max, do you even know where you're going?"

"Yeah, I do…but why not go ahead and ask her?" Max chuckled.

"I wouldn't do that if I were you," Ricky warned. I approached the cat anyway and discovered a much too bushy tail.

Ugh! A skunk!

"You might want to invest in some glasses, princess," Max's laughs grew louder.

I tried to back away but I wasn't quick enough. Spew! She sprayed me square in the face.

"I guess you scared her," Both Max and Ricky laughed. I gagged at my own stink. Shelby would smell me coming from a mile away!

Acting like it didn't bother me, with my head held high, I started to walk away but I didn't last long. Splat! I landed in another muddy puddle. Great. Max finally stopped laughing and helped me up.

"Thanks." I said with slight sass.

"Come on," he said looking me up and down in disgust, "Let's get you cleaned up."

I was going to have to accept. The smell was unbearable.

"You guys headed to Swamp Tizzy?" Ricky asked.

"Yep," said Max. "You coming?"

"Nah, man," Ricky answered. "I'm headed back to the trash alley; my time got cut short today and I'm starving!" He looked over at me and winked.

"Sorry," I said.

"It's no big deal," Ricky reassured me. "I'm happy to help. Be careful not to run into Albert at the swamp.." "Fingers crossed," Max said.

"Thanks again, Ricky!" I called.

"Not a problem! Bye Sandy, hope to see you soon," Ricky gave me a hug despite the mud and smell. Now, that was true friendship.

I liked my new friend Ricky but I really hoped that he was wrong. I didn't want to see him soon. I wanted to be at home, curled up with Shelby and enjoying as much food and clean water as I wanted. I watched him wander towards the alley, humming Taylor Swift again.

"Who's Albert?" I asked Max softly.

"Come on." He ignored me purposely. "Let's head down to the swamp."

Chapter 4

Running after Max was a workout and I was not in shape. He
led me to a huge lake before slowing down to look around.
"Oh good, the coast is clear. I don't think Albert is home so we
should be okay for a while."
"Who's Albert?" I asked again.
"You don't want to know," Max told me, jumping into the
water. I stood at the edge of the lake I looked down at my
reflection. I was a wreck. My favorite bow, the one Shelby
had given me the day we met, was gone. My fur was
straggly and clumped.
"What are you waiting for? Jump in! Don't be a scaredy-
cat," Max mocked.
I snapped out of it. He did not just call me a cat! SPLASH! I
launched myself into the freezing water. The chill took me
back to the night of the hurricane. I could hear Shelby
screaming and Kelly calling for Luke and I to swim back to the
boat. I paddled to the surface and gasped for air.

"Are you okay?" Max asked.

"I think so," I said. I wasn't. I turned around and saw a green scaly alligator swimming towards us. Max followed my gaze and spun.

"Uh-oh," Max dove underwater, leaving me to fend for myself. "Who are you and why are you here?" The alligator asked in a loud booming voice.

"I'm...I'm," I stuttered. Max came back up from the water and swam right up to the alligator.

"This is Sandy, Albert." Oh. So this was Albert. He didn't look nice at all.

"Max, I should've known it was you trespassing in my lake. Didn't I scare you enough last time you were down here with that dumb raccoon. Don't make me do that again in front of your lady friend."

In the time I've known Max, I've never seen him speechless, but he was now. He gulped. I stepped in.

"Sorry, I didn't know that we were trespassing. I thought this was a community lake. I just wanted to wash off my fur because I fell in some mud," I tried to explain. Albert was not having it. "Listen, little missy, I don't care what you wanted to do in my lake. This is private property. So you need to go."

"No it's not," Max interrupted. Albert shot him a look of disgust and pressed on.

"This IS private property," he said more firmly. "I WILL be pressing charges if you do not get off my property within the next ten minutes."

"Woah! There is no need to be so rude and definitely no need to press charges. We've done nothing wrong and I believe Max. There's no way that this is private property. Where are the signs?"

"I wouldn't get sassy with him, Sandy," Max tried to warn me. I waved him off. Albert started to turn away.

"You listen here," Albert turned back and I continued. "I was muddy, smelled like skunk, and, unlike you, I wanted to be clean. So SORRY."

"She did not just go there," Albert seethed. I glanced at Max who looked impressed. "Sandy, was it?" Albert asked. "Are you done? Can you just get out of my lake already?"

"Listen here, you slimy alligator," I snapped. Max stopped me. "Let's just go."

"No! He doesn't get to talk to us like we're not important!" "Please, Miss Sandy," Albert said slyly, "do go on." I did.

"I don't like your attitude, Albert, and you shouldn't treat people the way that you do. You think you can bully everyone into getting what you want because you're scary. Well, think again because I'm not scared of you and that's not how this works. Bullies never get anywhere in life. They just put other people down to feel better about themselves. In the end, you'll realize that you're alone because everyone got tired of you being so mean. If I want to swim in this lake, I will."

Albert and Max's mouths hung open, but I wasn't sorry. I'd seen bullies pick on Shelby before. I was not going to stand for it. I looked over at Max,

"Let's go. I'm clean now." I turned to Albert. "We're leaving because we want to," I told him, "not because you made us." Albert stood totally still and then, very slightly, he nodded his head in understanding and his jaw still hung open. Max and I exited the lake.

"That was crazy, Sandy," Max laughed. "You could have gotten us killed."

"He wouldn't have killed us. I've met people like him. They just want us to think that they're scary."

"Well, that was amazing," Max smiled at me.

"He's just lucky I didn't jaw him," I replied. Together, we headed away from the lake.

Chapter 5

Walking back, I thought about what I'd said to Albert and how lucky I probably was to be walking away at all. No bully was going to be the boss of me or my friends.

The stars shone bright and the moon was full. We walked slowly and ended up in a small park with a big playground. I could have sworn I heard Shelby's laugh but when I looked, all I saw was an empty slide and a couple of lonely swings swaying in the wind.
"We can sleep here tonight," Max said. I kept my eyes on the playground. "Guess you're not a princess afterall," Max told me after a long pause. I took a good look at my scraggly fur and laughed.
"I sure wish I looked like one."
"You do," Max whispered just loud enough for me to hear.
I smiled to myself. Max was actually kind of cute if you looked past his matted fur. I curled up and was getting ready to settle

down for the night when I saw him walking away.
"Where are you going," I asked.
"Aren't you hungry? I was going to grab something from
that trash can over there."

In next to no time, Max returned with a brown paper bag. He
tore it open. A half-eaten sandwich and an apple fell out. He
offered me first pick. I kindly declined. I would rather go
hungry than eat that.
"So, what's your deal?" I asked as he started chowing
down. "What do you mean my deal?" Bits of ham sandwich
splattered out of his mouth.
"Why do you act so tough on the outside when we all know
you're a big softy on the inside?" I laughed. Max fell quiet,
"Max?" I said. "I'm sorry. I didn't mean it like that. I just
wondered why you agreed to help me even though you didn't
want to?"
"It's complicated," Max said.
"Can you try to uncomplicate it for me? I'd really like to
know." Max let out a big sigh.
"I was once like you. I wasn't a service dog, but I used to be
loved and adored by a boy named Lance. The last time I saw
him was when he 5 years old. We used to play all day and
every night I would sleep in his arms. He was my boy and I
loved him very much." He took a moment to swallow the lump
I could hear building in his throat. "There was talk of a big
storm. Lance's mom and dad started panicking and preparing
to evacuate. The storm hit and they left, leaving me behind.

I got out of the house before the water got too high and started walking. This is where I ended up." "Oh my gosh, Max. I'm so sorry."

"Don't be sorry, Sandy. It made me who I am today. I've been on my own for a couple of years now and I like it that way. I think I'm better off alone anyway."

"No one should have to go through life on their own," I said softly.

"But I do," Max replied.

"No." I told him. "I'm here for you. I know we haven't known each other for long but I always will be here for you."

"Thanks," Max said sadly, "That means a lot to me." "It's the least I can do." I smiled.

"You know, I haven't told anyone that before. Not even Ricky." "I'm glad you trusted me." I watched him for a little while and wished with all my might that I would find Shelby soon. Then, finally, I fell asleep.

Chapter 6

The next morning, I woke close to Max who was still sleeping peacefully. Despite everything, I was starting to like him. We'd lived such different lives and were still so much alike. I nudged him awake and he opened his eyes and yawned. "Sorry to wake you up," I said.

"It's a good thing you did! We should probably get going, huh? The early bird catches the worm."

"You know what they say," I laughed. "When you're right, you're right."

Off we went. Down more twisting roads and twirling alleys. We laughed a lot and talked about everything. Max told me about his life on the streets and I told him all about Shelby, trying hard not to overdo it and make him jealous. We stopped at T-bones and ate some delicious steaks. Then, we headed out again until we finally came up to a big brown school building. I recognized it right away because I'd been coming to it for most of my life.

"I know where I am! I can get home from here," I shouted at Max who was trailing behind. "This is Shelby's school," I told him. I thought he'd be happy for me, but his head hung low, his bottom lip sticking out in a pout. "What's wrong," I asked.

"Now that you know where you are, you don't need me anymore," he snapped.

"What?" I asked.

"Nothing," he spat. "Princess service dog Sandy." I ignored his last comment and pressed on.

"When we get back to my house, you can live with us if you'd like," I said excitedly. I really hoped that he would accept my offer.

"No thanks, I'm good," Max muttered.

"Stop putting up your walls." I tried to walk closer to him, but he turned away and stared up at a nearby telephone pole.

"Let's just get there." He growled at me.

"No," I said, craning my neck to see what he was looking at. "Let's talk about it."

"There's nothing to say, Sandy," said Max. He dropped his head and started to walk away from me. Then I saw it. There was a missing dog poster nailed to the pole with a big picture o Shelby and I on it. "We come from two completely different places," Max said, "and that's that."

"Max…" I didn't know what to say to him. We walked up to the hill that led to my house.

"My house is just over this hill," I said. I was trying to be

sensitive, but I could barely contain my excitement. Max
followed me at a snail's pace. I caught sight of my home.
There wasn't much damage to the house except for a few
uprooted trees and a big mess of leaves. Luke and Kelly were
playing in the backyard. Shelby sat quietly on her swing
swaying back and forth. I couldn't help myself. I ran to them.
Max hung back.
"SANDY!" Shelby saw me first. I ran to her and jumped,
covering her white t-shirt in dirty footprints and licking at her
face. Luke ran over and hugged me too.
"Thank you," he told me, again and again. It made my
heart melt.
"Looks like you need a bath," Kelly laughed as I licked
her hand.
"I'm so glad you're back, Sandy," Shelby said happily, "I
missed you so much." She hugged as tightly as she could.

Max stood alone on the hill, looking down at us. He started to
turn away, his face drooped. Luke spotted him.

"Mommy, look! Sandy made a friend!" Luke ran to Max and threw his arms around him in a bear hug. Then, he led Max over to the rest of us. Shelby approached Max and gave him a hug too.

"He's got a collar on," she said. "He must belong to someone." She flipped the tag at his neck to read it. "That's weird. It just says 'Max.'"

"Nothing else? No phone number or address," Kelly asked. "Nope, nothing."

"Mommy, can we PLEASE keep him?" Luke begged. Kelly glanced between Max and Luke. "I don't think so honey," she said gently. I started to bark in outrage. Poor Max was trying hard not to cry.

"I'll fix this," I promised him. "You're not going anywhere, trust me!"

"It's fine, Sandy," Max said sadly. "Really, I understand. Who would want a dog like me anyway? I wasn't good for Lance. What makes me think that I'd be good for anyone else?" "You are good enough," I shouted.

"MOMMY! PLEASE!" Luke clung to Max tightly. "We'll take him to the shelter first thing in the morning," Kelly said. "I'm sorry, sweetie, we just can't keep him. It's too much with Shelby's condition. We're lucky to have Sandy back in our lives." I shot Shelby a look of sadness and she caught on right away.

"Mom, I'm fine. I think it would be okay if…." Shelby trailed off as her mom gave her a look and shook her head in disagree-ment.

"Come on let's go inside and get you both something to eat," Kelly said to Max and I, heading towards the back door. "You both look like you're starving." She wasn't wrong. I was hungrier than I'd ever been.

Shelby took me, and Luke carried Max into the house. I ate the biggest and best dinner of my life and felt a lot better. "Man, this stuff is way better than the trash I've been eating lately," Max chuckled, licking his bowl clean. Luke stayed close by and kept his eyes on Max. I watched Shelby work on her homework, humming her favorite Taylor Swift song as per usual. She was such a good girl! Man, I missed her.

When Max finished his dinner, we all went upstairs for a much-needed bath. Shelby washed me and Luke helped his mom wash Max. The warm water felt so good. I'd almost forgotten how great it felt to be clean! The bath water turned almost black. Gross! Shelby had to work hard to rinse all of the mud off of my legs. She tried her hardest to get the gum out of my fur.

"Sandy, I know you're going to be upset but I might have to cut some of your fur." I stared at her in disbelief. "It's going to be okay."

Max was having the time of his life, licking Luke's face and enjoying the chance to be a part of a family, even for a little while. I really wished he could stay with us, but I didn't see Kelly changing her mind any time soon. When bedtime came, I hugged Max tightly.

"It's going to be okay, Max," I told him.

He nodded his head and I headed into Shelby's room. I jumped on her bed and waited for her to come in. Shelby put her pajamas on and picked out the book that she was going to read to me like we did every night. Luke was throwing a fit like usual, but this time it actually wasn't about wanting to stay up later. It was about Max.

"Can he please sleep with me, Mommy?" Luke pleaded.

"No sweetie," Kelly said. "He's going to sleep in the basement. I've already made a bed for him down there." "But MOMMY!"

"The answer is no. I'm sorry." Kelly's voice was firm.

"But why?!"

"Luke, please stop."

Shelby shut her door, blocking out the noise, and crawled into bed with me.

"Oh Sandy, I missed you so much," she said as I nuzzled into her. She hugged me tightly. She started to stroke my head and she noticed that my bow was gone. "Where is your bow?" She asked. I started to whimper, "Oh Sandy. It's okay baby. We can get you another one," she smiled. With Shelby by my side, I knew everything would be alright. "I'm just so glad you're back. I love you so much!"

At times like these, I wished I could talk to Shelby in human language. I would tell her that I loved her and had missed her too. I would tell her everything! About crazy Ricky, about the skunk that I scared, about nasty Albert, and about how special Max was to me. I would tell Shelby how much I loved Max and that I couldn't bear to lose him. Instead, I listened to her read and watched her fall asleep.

Long after Kelly went to bed, I heard Luke moving around. "Come on buddy," I heard him whisper. Max's nails clicked against the wooden stairs, "You're such a good boy. Don't worry I'm going to talk to my mommy and we're going to keep you." I smiled. Then, finally, I fell into my first decent sleep since the storm washed me away.

Chapter 7

I woke up to the smell of eggs and bacon in the morning.
Shelby was already downstairs having breakfast. I passed
Luke's room as I headed downstairs, looking in through his
open door. They were both still asleep. Luke had one arm
around Max and Max was cuddled close to him. It was
adorable. I headed down to the kitchen where Kelly was on the
phone.
"I understand. Yes, we will be bringing him by later this
morning." I knew she was talking about Max and I started to
cry. Shelby ran to me and gave me a big hug just as Luke
came downstairs, hearing the conversation and bursting into
tears as well. As Shelby turned to hug Luke, I snuck back
upstairs.

"Sandy!" Max was awake and waiting for me. I pounced on
him and licked his nose. He laughed. "I guess someone's
excited

to see me!" I had a big grin on my face.

"How did you sleep?" I asked him.

"Amazing. Best night's sleep I've had in years! Luke's a great snuggle buddy and he talked to me all night about all kinds of stuff." Max looked truly happy. I could hardly cope with the idea of taking him to the shelter..

"I'm so happy that you like it here," I said.

"It's great," Max told me, "and I love Luke already. He told me everything! About Shelby and you. The best part is, he promised to let me stay! He said that I could be his dog!"

Later that day we all piled into the van. I sat on Shelby's lap and Luke held onto Max, barely keeping his sobs under control. Max licked his face to comfort him. When we arrived at the shelter, no one wanted to get out of the car. Kelly went to the front desk to talk to the staff. I felt Shelby's tears falling one by one onto my fur and I could see Max, cuddled in Luke's arms, trying hard not to cry.

The staff had to pull Max away from Luke before taking him to the back room. Both Luke and Shelby cried harder. Even Kelly looked upset. The whole way home, everyone sat in silence. Then, when we were almost back at the house, Kelly seemed to decide something. She turned to look at Luke.

"We're going back to get him." We turned around and headed straight back to the shelter to get Max. Kelly changed her mind. Thank goodness.

Max's face lit up when he saw Luke walk through the doors. He started to bark and jump and the window of the room he he was in.

"Max," Luke called out. "I'm here to save you, buddy."

Kelly talked with the staff and they quickly brought Max back out. I ran up to him and licked his face. Luke and Shelby followed behind me. He laughed.

"Oh thank goodness, Sandy."

"I'm so sorry that this happened," I told him.

"It's okay," he said. "I knew you'd come back. Luke promised."

When all the paperwork had been filled out, we finally piled back into the car, Luke holding Max in his arms and smiling from ear to ear. On the way home, we laughed and sang as loud as we could. "We Are Never Getting Back Together" came on the radio and I grinned, remembering Ricky. I had a crazy adventure, but it was worth it. I was so glad to be going home with Max. When we got home, we all ran inside, but Max stayed outside on the porch for a moment.

"What's wrong," I hung back with him.

"Nothing, Sandy," he said happily. "I'm just taking it all in." "Max! Come inside, we're waiting for you!" Luke shouted gleefully.

"It feels so good to finally have a place to call home," Max told me. He ran into the house, jumped on Luke, and licked his face "and to finally have a boy who loves me again."

Made in the USA
Monee, IL
31 July 2023